My "c" Sound Box®

(This book uses the hard "c" sound in the story line. Blends are included.
Words beginning with the soft "c" sound and the "c-h" sound
are included at the end of the book.)

Library of Congress Cataloging-in-Publication Data
Moncure, Jane Belk.
My "c" sound box / by Jane Belk Moncure; illustrated by Colin King.
p. cm.
Summary: A little girl fills her sound box with many words beginning with the letter "c."
ISBN 1-56766-769-4 (lib. bdg. : alk. paper)
[1. Alphabet.] I. King, Colin, ill. II. Title.
PZ7.M739 Myc 2000
[E]—dc21   99-055410

My "C"
Sound Box®

Jane Belk Moncure

illustrated by Colin King

The Child's World®

Little c had a box.

"I will find things that begin
with my 'c' sound," she said.

"I will put them into
my sound box."

Little **c** was cold.

She found some coats.

Little C put on a coat.

Did she put the other coats into her box?

She did.

Little found some caps.

She put on a cap.

Did she put the other caps into her box with the coats? She did.

Then Little saw a caterpillar.

Before she put the caterpillar into the box, it made a

So she put the cocoon into her box!

Soon Little  found a car.

She got into the car and went for a drive in the

country.

She saw a  cat.

The cat was chasing a canary.

13

Little  caught the cat.

She put it into her box.

She saw a  cat.

The cat was chasing a canary.

Little  caught the cat.

She put it into her box.

Then she called to the canary.
The canary flew into the cage.

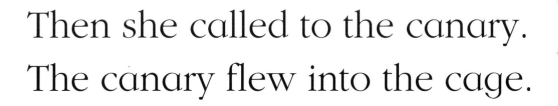

Little

put the cage and canary into her box.

Little 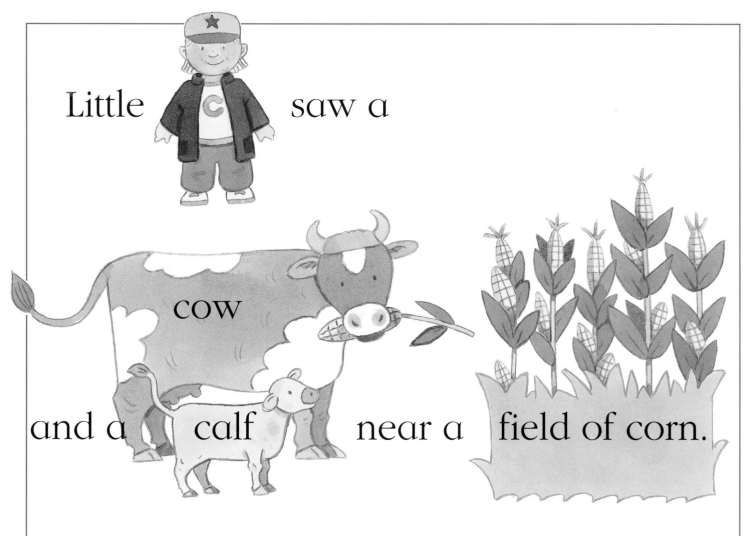 saw a

cow

and a calf near a field of corn.

She put the cow, the calf, and some corn into her box. Then . . .

Little  drove her car through a desert.

She saw a camel and a cactus.

She put them into her box. She drove to the end of the road, where she found a ...

castle!

A big castle.

A clown  was in the castle door.

"Come in," said the clown.

Little  got out of the car.

She carried her box into the castle.

She saw  candy canes,

cookies,

and a cake

with candles on it.

"You are just in time for my party!" said the clown.

Little ☐ took off her coat and cap.

She lifted the cage with
the canary out of the box.
She lifted out the cocoon
with the caterpillar inside.
Then all the other animals
came out of the box.

They all sat down
to a birthday party.

cow

calf

cage

canary

candy

candy canes

camel

cat

candles

clown

cookies

cake

The caterpillar did not eat, because it was still in the cocoon.

25

Can you read these words with Little  ?

crown

cotton candy

can

camera

curtain

carrot

cup

comb

cloud

card

crayon

cowboy

calendar

	1	2	3	4	5	6
7	8	9	10	11	12	13
14	15	16	17	18	19	20
21	22	23	24	25	26	27
28	29	30	31			

cucumber

cape

In the sound box story, Little C (hard) has

a hard sound—like the sound of the

letter "k." Little C (soft) has a soft sound,

too. The soft sound is like the sound of

the letter "s." Read these words with

Little C, and listen for the soft sounds.

circle

centipede

cigar

cent

celery

circus

cymbals

cereal

city

Little  can get together with the letter "h" to make still another sound. Can you read these words with the "c-h" sound?

chalkboard

chalk

chocolate

chimney

cherry

church

chicken

chipmunk

chain

ABOUT THE AUTHOR AND ILLUSTRATOR

Jane Belk Moncure began her writing career when she was in kindergarten. She has never stopped writing. Many of her children's stories and poems have been published, to the delight of young readers, including her son Jim, whose childhood experiences found their way into many of her books.

Mrs. Moncure's writing is based upon an active career in early childhood education. A recipient of an M.A. degree from Columbia University, Mrs. Moncure has taught and directed nursery, kindergarten, and primary grade programs in California, New York, Virginia, and North Carolina. As a former member of the faculties of Virginia Commonwealth University and the University of Richmond, she taught prospective teachers in early childhood education.

Mrs. Moncure has travelled extensively abroad, studying early childhood programs in the United Kingdom, The Netherlands, and Switzerland. She was the first president of the Virginia Association for Early Childhood Education and received its award for outstanding service to young children.

A resident of North Carolina, Mrs. Moncure is currently a full-time writer and educational consultant. She is married to Dr. James A. Moncure, former vice president of Elon College.

Colin King studied at the Royal College of Art, London. He started his freelance career as an illustrator, working for magazines and advertising agencies.

He began drawing pictures for children's books in 1976 and has illustrated over sixty titles to date.

Included in a wide variety of subjects are a best-selling children's encyclopedia and books about spies and detectives.

His books have been translated into several languages, including Japanese and Hebrew. He has four grown-up children and lives in Suffolk, England, with his wife, three dogs, and a cat.

My "n" Sound Box

Library of Congress Cataloging-in-Publication Data
Moncure, Jane Belk.
My "n" sound box / by Jane Belk Moncure; illustrated by Colin King.
p. cm.
Summary: A little girl fills her sound box with many words beginning with the letter "n."
ISBN 1-56766-780-5
[1. Alphabet.] I. King, Colin, ill. II. Title.
PZ7.M739 Myn   2000
[E]—dc21   99-054329

My "n" Sound Box®

Jane Belk Moncure

illustrated by Colin King

The Child's World®

Little  had a box.

"I will find things that begin
with my 'n' sound," she said.

"I will put them into my sound box."

Little n found a tree with nuts on it.

Little  climbed the tree.
She picked nuts.

How many nuts?

8

Little  counted nine nuts.

She made the number 9.

Did she put the nuts and the number 9 into her box? She did.

Next, Little  n made nine groups of nuts.

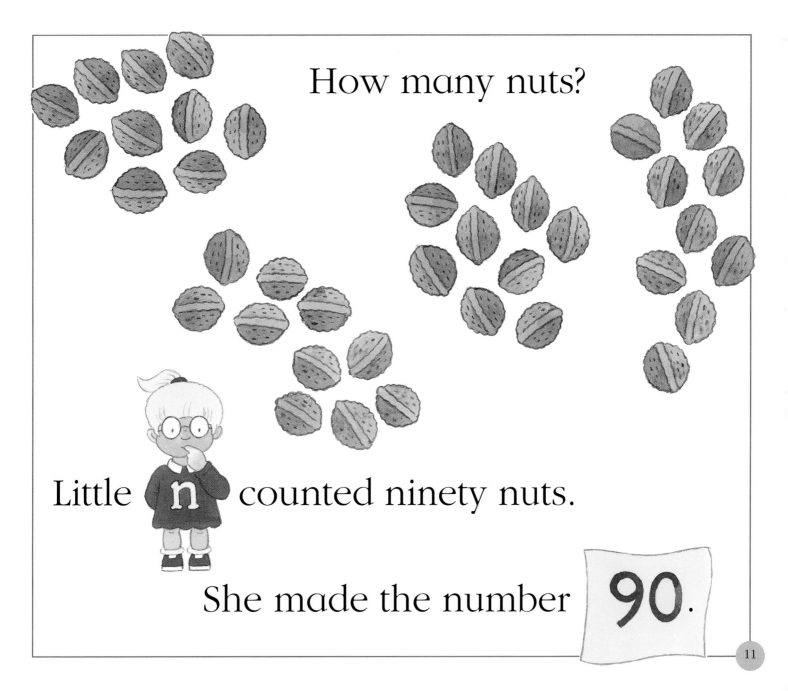

How many nuts?

Little n counted ninety nuts.

She made the number 90.

She put these nuts into her box with the other nuts. Now how many nuts did she have?

Little **n** counted ninety-nine nuts.

She made the number 99.

Did she put the number 99 into her box? She did.

Then Little n climbed the tree again.

Little n found nightingales . . .

nine nightingales
eating nuts!

15

When the nightingales saw

Little n,

they flew into
their nests.

Little  put the nightingales
and their nests
into her box,

carefully . . .

because there were eggs in the nests.

Little **n** could not count how many.

next day, Little  got out her

ay bank.

emptied out

nickels . . .

Little  n was sleepy.

So she took a nap.

The
pigg
She
her

The next day, Little  got out her piggy bank.
She emptied out
her nickels . . .

Little  n was sleepy.

So she took a nap.

lots of nickels, 99 nickels!

Little  n took her nickels to a store.

She bought a necklace for her mother

and a necktie for her father.

She also bought a nutcracker.

Little  had 19 nickels left.

So she bought a nightgown for herself.

Little  carried all her

new things home.

She put on her new nightgown.

Then she heard a noise.
She looked into her box and saw
nineteen new nightingales.

They were crying for nuts!

"Don't cry," said Little  n.
"I have enough nuts
    for all of you."
She cracked some nuts.

nightingales

nests

nuts

nuts

While the nightingales ate,
she spread out her new things.

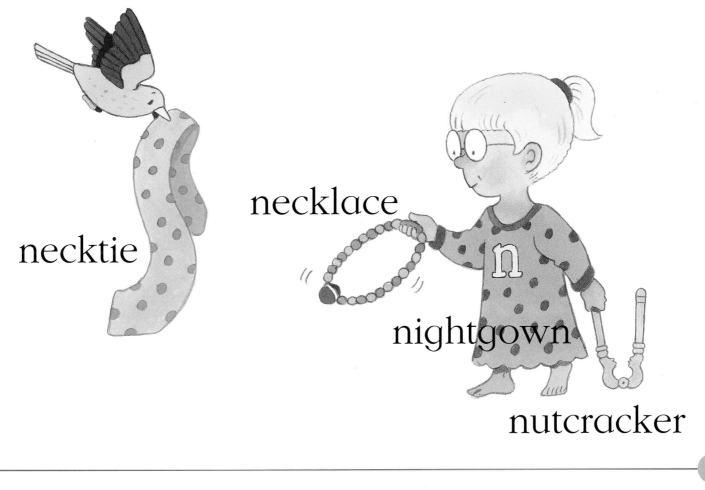

necktie

necklace

nightgown

nutcracker

Can you read these words with Little n ?

nectarine

newspaper

noodles

nose

notes

needle

28

nail

napkin

November

1	2	3	4	5	6	7
8	9	10	11	12	13	14
15	16	17	18	19	20	21
22	23	24	25	26	27	28
29	30					

nurse

narcissus

net

ABOUT THE AUTHOR AND ILLUSTRATOR

Jane Belk Moncure began her writing career when she was in kindergarten. She has never stopped writing. Many of her children's stories and poems have been published, to the delight of young readers, including her son Jim, whose childhood experiences found their way into many of her books.

Mrs. Moncure's writing is based upon an active career in early childhood education. A recipient of an M.A. degree from Columbia University, Mrs. Moncure has taught and directed nursery, kindergarten, and primary grade programs in California, New York, Virginia, and North Carolina. As a former member of the faculties of Virginia Commonwealth University and the University of Richmond, she taught prospective teachers in early childhood education.

Mrs. Moncure has travelled extensively abroad, studying early childhood programs in the United Kingdom, The Netherlands, and Switzerland. She was the first president of the Virginia Association for Early Childhood Education and received its award for outstanding service to young children.

A resident of North Carolina, Mrs. Moncure is currently a full-time writer and educational consultant. She is married to Dr. James A. Moncure, former vice president of Elon College.

Colin King studied at the Royal College of Art, London. He started his freelance career as an illustrator, working for magazines and advertising agencies.

He began drawing pictures for children's books in 1976 and has illustrated over sixty titles to date.

Included in a wide variety of subjects are a best-selling children's encyclopedia and books about spies and detectives.

His books have been translated into several languages, including Japanese and Hebrew. He has four grown-up children and lives in Suffolk, England, with his wife, three dogs, and a cat.